THE LONG WAY TO A NEW LAND

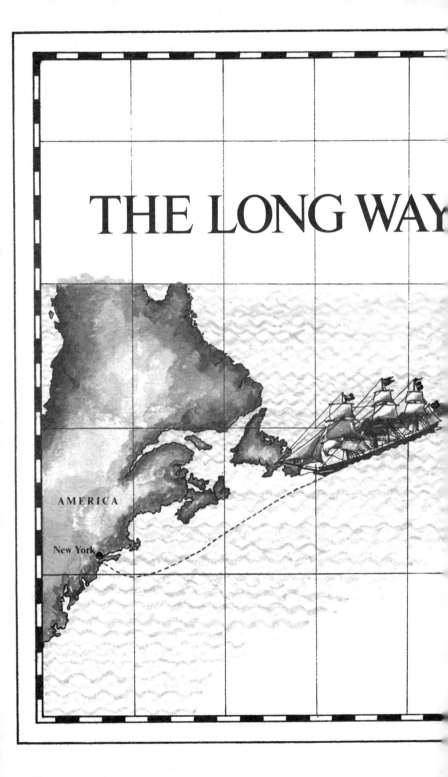

THE LONG WAY

AMERICA

New York

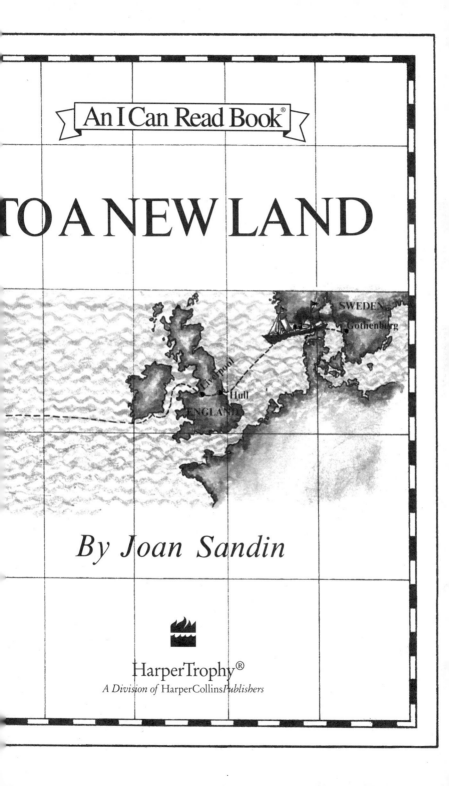

An I Can Read Book®

TO A NEW LAND

SWEDEN
Gothenburg

Liverpool
Hull
ENGLAND

By Joan Sandin

HarperTrophy®
A Division of HarperCollins*Publishers*

The Long Way to a New Land
Copyright © 1981 by Joan Sandin
All rights reserved. No part of this book may be used or reproduced in any manner
whatsoever without written permission except in the case of brief quotations embodied
in critical articles and reviews. Printed in the United States of America. For information
address HarperCollins Children's Books, a division of HarperCollins Publishers,
10 East 53rd Street, New York, NY 10022.

Library of Congress Cataloging-in-Publication Data
Sandin, Joan.
    The long way to a new land.

    (An I can read history book)
    Summary: Carl Erik journeys with his family from
Sweden to America during the famine of 1868.
    [1. United States—Emigration and immigration—
Fiction. 2. Sweden—Emigration and immigration—
Fiction] I. Title. II. Series: I can read history
book.
PZ7.S217Lo   1981   [E]   80-8942
ISBN 0-06-025193-X   AACR2
ISBN 0-06-025194-8 (lib. bdg.)
ISBN 0-06-444100-8 (pbk.)

CONTENTS

For Sigfrid

I. THE LETTER FROM AMERICA

Carl Erik's father shook his fist

at the clear blue sky.

"Rain!" he cried.

"We must have rain!"

But the rain did not come.

The whole summer passed

without a drop of rain.

The grass dried up.

The cow could not give milk.

The crops did not grow.

There would be no food

for the long winter.

Carl Erik and his brother Jonas

gathered moss in the forest.

They scraped bark from pine trees.

Mamma mixed it with flour

to bake their bread—

a hard and bitter bread

that made their stomachs ache.

Pappa tried to buy food.

"It is hopeless," he told Mamma.

"There is nothing to buy.

People have left their farms.

I saw children begging."

11

One day a letter came

from Uncle Axel in America.

12

Dear ones,

The worst is now over.

It is a new life for us here.

We have built our house.

Our land is good.

We will have food for the winter.

We think of you there in Sweden.

We know how hard it must be.

Your farm is small and rocky.

You have three sons.

What future do they have?

Come! We will help you.

Come to America!

Carl Erik saw something

on the back of Uncle Axel's letter:

Dear Carl Erik
We have a cow and
twelve chickens. We eat
wheat bread with butter
every day. I have seen
an Indian. He was not
fierce. I can speak
English better than
Mamma and Pappa!
Your cousin Anna Stina

"I want wheat bread with butter,"

said Jonas.

"Can we go to America?"

That night Carl Erik

could not sleep.

He was too hungry.

He was thinking

of Anna Stina's letter.

He could hear Mamma and Pappa

talking in their bed.

They were still talking

when Carl Erik finally fell asleep.

The next morning Pappa said,

"There is no future for us here.

We will go to America."

II. GOOD-BYE TO SWEDEN

There were many things to do
before they could leave.
Mamma took all the flour
and baked hard flat bread.
She washed the quilts.
She sewed new clothes.

Pappa made a big trunk with a lock.
He sold their small farm
and most of their things.
He did not get much money.
But it was enough
to buy their tickets to America.

19

They filled the "America trunk"
with homespun cloth, tools,
Pappa's rifle and the Bible.
"Can I take Pontus?" asked Jonas.
"Yes," said Pappa, "one toy each."

Carl Erik rolled up the bedding.
He and Jonas packed the cups,
bowls and spoons.
Mamma put cheese, dried meat
and bread into a big basket.
She packed the copper coffeepot.

21

They said good-bye to the people
they had known all their lives.
Farmor hugged her grandsons.
"My poor darlings," she said.

Her cheeks were wet with tears.

Jonas hopped away from *Farmor.*

He was too excited to hold still.

Carl Erik and Jonas took turns

riding on the cart.

They saw many other people.

"Emigrants," said Pappa,

"just like us."

They met at the inns each night.

They talked about America.

They shared their plans and hopes

for a better life

in a new land.

It took three days to reach

the seaport city of Gothenburg.

"Look at the high houses!"

shouted Jonas.

"Look at the sails

on the boats!" said Carl Erik.

Pappa sold the cart and horses

and bought their tickets.

The boat would leave the next day.

They waited with the other emigrants
until the mailbags, lumber
and cattle were loaded.
Then they went on board.

"Good-bye Sweden!" said Mamma.

"Good-bye forever!" cried Pappa.

III. FOUR DAYS TO LIVERPOOL

It was smelly and dark

under the deck.

People were packed together

on the benches.

They were lying on the floor.

"Where will we sleep?" asked Mamma.

Pappa found a place for them

by the engine room.

"It is noisy here," he said,

"but it is only for three nights."

Every morning Mamma waited in line

to boil water for their coffee.

Then she carefully divided up

the cheese and bread.

31

Three days later

they docked in Hull.

"Is this America?" asked Jonas.

"No," said Pappa. "This is England.

They speak English here."

But the first person they met

spoke Swedish.

He was an emigrant agent

from the steamship company.

He helped them with their baggage

and got them safely

to the railway station.

The train to Liverpool

hissed and tooted

and click-clacked its way

across the English countryside.

It passed fields and meadows

and rows of brick houses.

It went in and out of tunnels

and by factories puffing dirty smoke.

That night they slept in beds

in an emigrant hotel.

The Liverpool port was crowded.

The Swedish families

huddled together.

Carl Erik held on tightly

to Pappa's hand.

All around him

he heard the strange languages

of other emigrants:

English, German, Norwegian,

Italian, French.

The emigrants boarded the ship.

A doctor examined them.

He looked

for their smallpox vaccinations.

An old woman

and a girl with a rash

were sent back to land.

40

Pappa found their bunks

in the section for families.

"Clean straw!" said Mamma.

She stuffed the mattresses

and laid out the bedding.

When the ship was loaded and ready,

the first-class passengers got on.

The doctor smiled at them.

The stewards helped them

to their cabins on deck.

Suddenly there was a roar of steam

and a clang of bells.

The *City of Baltimore*

was on her way to America.

IV. STORM AND FEVER

That evening

a steward placed

a kettle of fish stew

on the long table.

The emigrants dipped into the pot

with their cups and bowls.

They pushed and bumped each other.

A man next to Carl Erik

dipped into the pot

with his dirty hands.

CRASH!

Carl Erik woke up with a start.

An oil lamp had fallen to the floor.

The ship was rocking.

Seawater was everywhere.

Trunks slid around

on the wet floor.

Carl Erik was afraid.

He felt Pappa next to him in bed.

That was better.

He could hear people being sick.

The smell was terrible.

47

The storm raged for three days.

The emigrants were locked in.

No one could come up on deck.

Hundreds of voices

prayed and sang and cried.

Mamma and Jonas could not eat.

They became weak and feverish.

One night a hatch was unlocked.

A man climbed out.

He was carrying a small bundle.

The ship's bell rang.

"What is it?" asked Carl Erik.

"Someone has died," whispered Pappa.

The next day the sea was calm.

The crew unlocked the hatches.

They washed down the emigrant deck.

Meals were served once more.

Pappa helped Mamma and Jonas

to come up on deck.

They breathed in the fresh sea air.

They felt alive again.

A man sat down beside Pappa.

"It was much worse

before the steamships," he said.

"It took months then.

I know.

I have made this trip many times."

"Can you speak English?"

asked Carl Erik.

"English I am talking very good,"

said the man.

He showed Pappa a little book

called *Handbook for the Emigrant.*

"Everything you need to know

about the United States of America

and the English language," he said.

"I wrote it myself."

Every day Pappa and Carl Erik read

from *Handbook for the Emigrant.*

They memorized the English phrases:

What o'clock is it?

What country are you of?

Now we are arrived.

V. AMERICA AT LAST!

On the twelfth day

someone shouted, "LAND!"

The emigrants crowded up on deck

to see the New York coast.

"THIS is America!" cried Jonas.

"Yes," said Mamma. "At last!"

They packed their things

and dragged them up on deck.

They tore open their mattresses

and threw the straw overboard.

A tugboat pulled up alongside.

A health officer stepped aboard.

He talked to the captain.

"All clear for landing," he said.

56

The crew poked and pushed
the emigrants into lines.
"Hold hands!" Mamma shouted.
"We must not lose each other!"

Men in uniforms
examined their baggage.
A doctor looked into their eyes
and down their throats.
He thumped on their chests.
The lines moved slowly.
The baby was crying.

"I'm hungry," Jonas whined.

"I want wheat bread with butter."

"Be quiet," hissed Carl Erik.

His own legs ached from standing.

He watched the men

check Pappa's papers.

They asked him many questions—

first in English, then in Swedish.

He saw that Pappa was nervous.

58

Finally it was over!

They found a place to sit down.

"Don't move from here," said Pappa.

When he came back,

Pappa was laughing.

"Jonas," he said, "look!

Wheat bread with butter!"

But Jonas was fast asleep.

"We have a letter too!" said Pappa.

"Axel and Sara and Anna Stina

welcome us to America.

They will be at the railway station.

Everything is arranged,

and I have work for the winter!"

"Oh, Anders!" Mamma sighed.

"Soon we will have a home again."

61

Carl Erik looked around him

at the huge room.

Long lines of emigrants

were still waiting.

He heard their many languages.

He tasted the fresh wheat bread

and sweet butter

of his new land.

He leaned against Pappa's shoulder

and whispered,

"Now we are arrived."

AUTHOR'S NOTE

During the "hunger years" of 1868 and '69, more than 50,000 Swedes emigrated to America. Good farmland, jobs, social mobility, religious and political freedom drew them here. Newspapers, pamphlets and letters from earlier emigrants spread the *Amerikafeber*, or America fever. Like thousands of European emigrants of the time, the Swedes were willing to leave everything for the dream of a better life in the "land of opportunity."

Steamship travel made the trip shorter and safer than before, and there were handbooks (with their strange-sounding English-phrase dictionaries) written by Swedish "Yankees" to guide their fellow countrymen on their long way to a new land.